The TwoCent Times 1

An Anthology of Oddness

N MANTHEY

|

B C WOODRUFF

The TwoCent Times

SHATTER BOOKS

www.bcwoodruff.com

THE JOURNEY AHEAD

A Bit Too Fit

Mert walks south, and in his wake the day is leaving the world.

His footsteps are heavy and he trots more than he steps, with a precision that suggests he has been at this for a long, long time. The clouds, cascading against the azure blues of a bright midday sky, seem to suggest that there is yet a state of peace here. It is, of course, a lie.

Peace has never been a practical value for the corporation. Mert has always been aware of that and, perhaps, this is why it has been so difficult for him to appreciate the gravity of the gift they have given him. Well, they call it a gift. He knows better that it is something far more sinister and absurd. He's been getting fatter at his desk. Eating more of his rations and sneaking more whenever there's an opportunity.

This has not gone unnoticed, however.

At 152 kilograms, Mert is one particularly large human being. His bulbous form, reminiscent of an onion mixed with Jello, ripples under his movements. Jiggles find their way up to his breasts which are, likewise, swollen and sore from making his way so far from his home. So far, too, from his place of work and worship.

But it is necessary, he's been told.

Otherwise he will be sentenced and sent off to a bootcamp for reassessment and the stories of those places are far more traumatic than he cares to experience. So, instead, he's taken the corporation's direction to heart.

He's been equipped with a 'Fitter.' A device that monitors his movement. His heart rate. His breathing and his food intake. It takes into account his every physical action from the moment it was implanted onward. Connected through the digital mainframe to his doctor's office, it has access to all the visits he's had. All of the sicknesses in his past. All of his potential genetic complications. Everything that he is.

It is the latest and greatest (they say) of all health companions.

Epigeneticists have crafted it alongside the allmind to offer those that have it installed the advice and the information they need to become better. In taking into account each component of his life and surroundings, the Fitter provides the necessary recommendations for improving health and orients its host with personalized guidance. The intention is simple: a better existence for you and for your children.

But Mert has been walking and walking and feels the sun beating him down and wonders, rightfully so, when the damn thing will let him rest.

Because there is *that*, too.

The Fitter 'incentivises' the host with achievements and applause when you *obey* it. However, it also offers small bursts of chemical reactions in the brain should you decide *not* to heed its orders.

So, he walks on.

And on.

His face is chipping from the sunburn. Flakes fall down like disgusting snow onto the pavement behind him. A guide to bring him home like Hansel and Gretel. He imagines that delicious house with the witch inside. He'd eat them all if he had a chance. He'd drink the lakes bare in his state.

Still, he continues to follow the path the Fitter has set for him. He does not need a map or directions. His mind seems to *know* where to go. It's like birds migrating, he assumes, and ignores the implications there. Or, perhaps, it's more like salmon moving back up their rivers.

= Daily Quota Nearly Achieved! = The Fitter lets him know after many more steps forward and more of his face left trailing backwards, shimmering with blood and sweat in the twilight. He doesn't seem to mind this, though. The Fitter is rewarding him with smooth serotonin waves. He feels good, despite his legs pinching with each foot forward.

The sun sneaks away, but he's still walking.

A forest surrounds him as he continues along the way. Somehow, it doesn't seem that bad, this working out! He's content and pleased, even the blood and pus that's seeping from his wounds are of no concern.

The trees open to a field.

This is when the horror hits him.

Bodies, rotten and decayed, scattered everywhere.

A gale of death.

But even in the terror, he feels somewhat relieved.

= Goal Completed! = The Fitter tells him, but the voice is distant. More chemicals mask his pain.

He lies down and closes his eyes, pleased to rest.

A*MESH

Darkness.

No, not quite darkness.

A dizzying, infinite vacuum, scattered with the energy of distant stars. Luminescent grids danced over the field, crackling with heathen, unfathomable symbols and numbers. They beckoned, seeming to promise a clarity of understanding that would hold the key to untold worlds, if only they could be reached. The revelation was just a fraction of a second away...

Levi snapped back into consciousness, gasping. Another nightmare. And given its content, this one will have to be reported to the Elders.

Gingerly, he lowered his feet to the floor, waiting for the horror of the nightmare to pass, praying for the purity to return to his heart. To help restore the inner balance that he knew should be innate to all Amesh, Levi looked around the simple furnishings of his apartment, giving thanks to the Creator for the rustic, utilitarian objects among which he passed his life.

“By the grace of the Creator, I am one with the Earth,” he whispered fervently.

As often happened, Levi couldn’t resist peering out from beneath his half-closed eyelids, reassuring himself that the seductive symbols from his dreams have not followed him into reality. It’s a sin to doubt the ability of the Creator to protect him from Evil, but Levi can’t help it. The symbols have followed him through his daily Purifications often enough that he has started to wonder if he’s one of the Cursed. Flashes of impossibility during Worship, a distracting sequence of numbers at the zenith of labour, these were unsettling intrusions into an otherwise placid life. An idyllic life, some might call it.

Levi was acutely aware that he belonged to the chosen race. As was only natural, the Amesh rejected the decadence of the technological age, and eschewed the flaccid, yet robotic state currently favoured by most humans. How could one possibly be happy when reality existed only in fleeting pixels? It was insubstantial. Unnatural.

The Amesh knew that simplicity was the key to existence. Working with the earth, coaxing the precious gifts of the Creator from seeds and roots, demonstrating complete devotion to a single purpose. Those were the true elements of joy. Of fulfillment.

Savouring the feeling of permanence from the rough wool of his tunic and familiar embrace of his work boots, Levi dressed slowly. A sense of warm contentment, originating in his chest, soon radiated outward with almost mathematical precision, erasing the knots of anxiety and tension caused by those heathen numbers. All was right. Of course the Creator would protect him.

He set off towards the chapel, where morning Worship would soon commence. The milky grey of dawn cast an absurd, wintry pall over the landscape, suggesting the illusion that the buildings and fields were wrapped in a thin film of snow. Levi knew this impression was ludicrous, since the last snowfall had occurred more than ten years before his birth 21 years ago. With effort, he pushed the image aside, and fell in with the file of his fellow Amesh. Two by two, a measured tread. An effortless diurnal rhythm. No need for the clamorous peal of church bells. All Amesh were regulated by the precision of the Creator.

In the chapel, wrapped up in his private devotion, Levi sensed the familiar trickle of Instructions filtering into his conscious mind. Worship was much more than a repetition of prayers and supplications. It was a reiteration of the single, holy purpose that shaped the existence of the Amesh: producing the food that nourished their community. It was also a practical and efficient way to ensure no labour was wasted. By the grace of the Creator, every Amesh left the chapel with their daily task list firmly established. Levi relaxed into the familiar rhythm of the service, visualizing the labours ahead. With a sickening lurch, he became aware of a vibrant stream of numbers trailing along the lower edge of his perspective. Luminescent. Green. Mocking. His clasped hands began to shake. *Please Creator, no. Not here. Anywhere but here.*

Outside the chapel, Levi paused for a moment, struggling to regain his composure.

"Levi! Are you alright?" A gnarled hand on his shoulder.

“Yes, thank you David, I’m fine,” Levi responded, hoping his words sounded convincing.

David’s dark eyebrows furrowed slightly he scanned Levi’s face, searching. “Another nightmare?” he asked, gently.

Levi’s shoulders slumped. “Yes.”

“About time to see the Elders, I’d say, my boy. Do me a favour -- make it a priority after labour. In the meantime, I’ll be praying for you.” David raised the brim of his hat slightly, and with a meaningful look, turned towards his assigned section of field.

“Thanks David, I will,” Levi called after the departing figure. With a deep breath, he set off towards the far side of the compound, relishing the idea of a brisk walk before setting about his tasks. The Creator always knows. And provides.

To rid himself of the disquiet produced by the intrusion of evil into Worship, Levi began a standard contemplation on the bounty of the Creator. As a result of their simplicity and devotion, the Creator had rewarded the Amesh with robust health, limitless strength, a blissful state of contentment, and a secure place to live, untouched by the violence of the technological world. Perched in the centre of the continent, Levi took satisfaction in being isolated from the bitter CorpWars that raged from Flor on the west coast, to Amica in the east. He was only peripherally aware of the consuming greed that caused the various Corps to pervert the gifts of the Creator, using them to create weapons, drugs, enhancements, alterants, and other agents of human sickness and misery. And all for the sake of whichever bloated bureaucrat possessed the most credits. He shook his head. What a tragic way to live.

Soothed by the contrast, Levi soon lost himself in the ecstacy of labour. A rhythmic diving, delving of the multitool into the embracing earth. The reassuring *thuck, thuck* that filled his ears as each blow fell with precision. A divine smell of wet soil and burgeoning life, blessed by the rains of the night before. The supreme satisfaction of living by sweat and strength, untainted by illness, desire, or infectious complexity.

Unbidden, a sinking dread rose from the pit of his stomach. That meeting with the Elders. A confession. What if they think he's a Cursed? Everyone knows the Cursed simply cease to exist. Just last year, seven members of other Amesh compounds had vanished due to uncontrollable anti-Creator sentiments. And it always starts with questions, with uncertainty. Why does each community produce more food than it's capable of consuming? Why are we forbidden to leave the compound? Why must every Amesh devote themselves, body and soul, to the Creator and the fruits of the earth?

Hush. No more of these impure thoughts. The Creator sees the true soul of every Amesh. *Trust in the Creator, and all will be well.* There is no room for “why” in this existence. Just like there is no room for meaningless symbols and destructive numbers.

Flushed with the pleasure of his exertions, Levi surveyed his patch of field with satisfaction.

Looks like another bountiful harvest ahead, thank the Creator, he thought.

Th4nk th3 CreAto…

7h3 Cr3AtOr…

The…

Liquid fire scorched through Levi's veins as he collapsed onto the damp earth. A searing grid of symbols branded into the cloudless sky. Getting closer, overwhelming his sight. Growing darkness. Panic. Fear.

A message, dancing across his vision: "A*MESH Corporation: Food Production Unit LEVI 1589-A, Software v 8.0 -- critical failure. Initializing Elder Rescue Protocol 12-387."

Utter blackness. Familiar voices bubbling up from the depths. The Elders spoke to him in his dying hour. Maybe everything was going to be OK.

"Damned LEVI unit blew out on us again. It's a wonder these patched-together mecha-bio sons of bitches manage to grow anything with this glitchy code. Worst idea to ever come out of the Ag Department, I can tell you. Well, plug him in, and let's run

CREAT-R again. Maybe he'll work this time around."

No...

Spoiled

Being *Stateless*, that is, having been declared unfit for citizenship in Auro is nearly the same as being sentenced to death.

I had to collect my belongings at Four Winds Laboratory before my shift ended. I was escorted out by the Sector Lead and members of the Security Annex. There wasn't any time to speak with my friends. I complied, though, and walked out with a sense of optimism despite this new and frustrating change in my life.

My father, Delkirk Smithe, was waiting for me near the tram station.

"I received a notice from your estate." He's taller than I am and his aged face, with its various wrinkled trenches seemed even more upset than usual.

"I wasn't expecting to see you." Which is the truth. We haven't seen one another since I was bonded to Melina Prints, a woman working in the Centre for Acquisitions. It was because of Melina more than the Centre, really. But prior to the collapse in our relationship we'd been fighting for years. The realization that I was going to be bonded with *anyone* from Auro's banks was enough for him to decide he could slip out of contact with a resolve that his justifications were valid. Or, perhaps it was that he finally recognized that he could separate himself from me and be socially virtuous and not have to explain to the rest of the family why I would no longer be attending any of our gatherings.

I wanted to... he just couldn't accept the idea that I chose to bond with Melina. My mother and I have kept in light contact, but I haven't seen her or my younger sister in person for years.

"You know..." He starts. "I tried to contact you after I heard about Melina."

I assume he's lying. But I try to stay amicable. "I appreciate that."

"Terrible people, those Prints. I knew they weren't to be trusted." This much is true. He always warned my sister and I about people working at the Centre, particularly those who were Stateless as children.

"I know you did. If you remember, I had some reservations about bonding but her mother was very insistent."

"A shame you couldn't find someone like *your* mother. Of course, she was a rare sort. I told her that when we met. Just as we would eventually agree that Stateless children, generally, are only trying to make life better for themselves… I just can't understand how you would let Melina get away with all of *this*. Such a mess. Such a regrettable mess. If only you'd listened to us." His voice croaked and groaned.

"It just happened."

"But *how*?"

"I didn't notice my contributions were being moved around. By the time I had to provide the bank with payment... Well, it was too late."

"And you have nothing left?"

I nodded. In the distance steam was peaking above the tram walls. Soon, I would board it. Soon, I would have to leave Auro and never return. I didn't want to squabble with my old man.

"Nothing."

His head sank.

"What if your mother and I gave you a loan? Couldn't you talk to the Centre?"

"The verdict is final. I tried to offer insight into the situation to the law scribe but he just shrugged and sent me along my way. She probably paid him off, too."

"Your mother heard from her colleague at the Deportation Bureau that your case was one of the swiftest they'd ever seen go through. Just *what* were you working on when this happened?"

I couldn't tell him. "Nothing too interesting. We shouldn't go any further than that."

The tram arrived, all whistles and moving metal, slowing into a spot on the platform ahead. Behind me, the two security escorts were getting ready to force me in if I didn't go voluntarily.

"This is the end, I suppose." I shrugged and was caught completely off-guard when my father wrapped his arms around me for a hug. One that I needed more then than I could have realized. He whispered into my ear something that struck me even harder in the gut.

I was young again, at home, with him and mom and my sister. We were smiling and laughing at something here or there and I could smell the food in the kitchen. My mother, as always, was working on a new set of contributions, hoping that these would earn her a permanent state in the Auro Conceptrium.

My father was telling us a story about the places beyond Auro.

He told us, often, about his grandfather and how he had been admitted into Auro as an exception after the Candlestick War in the east. It was a point of pride that he, alone, out of twenty-five potentials made it through the stages to earn a state at the Centre. His position there was precisely the reason my father would come to distrust any of the Stateless children. That's a longer story, though.

His whisper into my ear reminded me of where we came from – and where I might go – out in the east.

There's another city, one far less sophisticated in comparison to Auro, but one that has managed to successfully repel their attacks and demands for contribution tithes.

He finished with: "Your mother has arranged for supplies near the crossroad next to Felmeck. Go to the travel lodge and ask for *Siam.*"

I'd held a lot of disdain against him and my mother after the bonding with Melina. Mostly, I suppose I had recognized how correct they had been about her and the situation. It was gone now.

I didn't imagine it would be that easy to wash off years of repressed hatred.

“I love you. And Mom. And Lorain.” I tell him and feel a prod from one of the security members behind me.

“We’ll meet again. I’m certain.” He tells me as I step into the disciplinary carriage with others that are being exiled.

He vanishes moments after the tram starts running down the track.

We move underground for a while. Passing flashes of light are all that lends itself to indicate we’re accelerating at all. Everyone is quiet, and in the darkness it seems appropriate.

Some time later we come out into the daylight again.

I can see Auro in the distance behind us.

The City of Silver, they call it, and from here it lives up to that description.

In the opposite direction is the Final Wall, a vertical structure that wraps the city in a protective and dangerous field that can only be entered or exited via the tram or if you're wearing a polarizing suit. We'll be outside soon, and then they'll let us out into the world.

Where we'll go – that doesn't matter to them. Only that we'll be gone and it will be impossible to return.

Thinking of Melina, I wonder if she has any regret or empathy for what she has done to me.

The tram comes to a stop a few hundred metres from the Final Wall.

"You will get out at the other side of the field. You have five minutes. After such time the tram's polarizing shield will be turned off and any still inside will suffer death. Do not return. You are no longer welcome in Auro." He pulled out a small metal cylinder the length of his palm and wrapped his hand around it. “Present your wrists.”

He walks through the cabin, pressing the flat edge against the skin, burning on a symbol for those who have been deemed Stateless. Coming to me he stops for a moment.

“You’re…”

“Yes.” I nod.

“Such a tragedy to see you go, sir.” He probably feels odd speaking respectfully to a Stateless – probably as odd as I feel, too.

“It couldn’t be helped.” I hold my wrist out and I can see him hesitate as he brings the cold metal against it.

“Stick to the roads. Don’t let people see this, either. They’ll take advantage of you. Try to make it to one of the western settlements.

I'm told there are lots of Stateless there. It'll be safer." He's speaking quietly but enough that a few others are listening to him and he catches this, changing back to a sterner tone.

"I wish you all life." He adds, continuing along to the next and the next, leaving them branded.

He exits the tram with the other guards. They won't be needed. The tram starts up and my hair starts to stand on its end, coinciding with the polarizing field coming into power. The Final Wall ahead is a blue shimmer at best, with shining points of metal that are probably keeping the energy flowing across the whole section. It's said that the Final Wall, when at full strength, takes nearly ninety percent of all the power generated from the thermal stations. Stories say that it vaporizes whatever comes in contact with it, even on its lower settings. One could certainly imagine the effect it would have at full power... terrifying as that would be.

We pass through the edge with a flurry of shocks sent through some of the less isolated areas in the corner, catching a small man off-guard enough that his hair bursts into blue flames that die out almost as quickly. Not quickly enough, however, leaving his hair reduced to ash with a searing wound steaming from his scalp. It's all happened in such a short period that only now, whole seconds later, has he started screaming.

The tram pulls up to a derelict station and the doors open.

There's no warning. No reminder of what will happen if we stay. Still, the other passengers are surprisingly collected as they move out in orderly lines, some already heading off in the direction of the setting sun. Possibly because they have heard what the officer said as he was branding us.

Not me, though.

I've stepped off the tram but I can't find the strength to move at all.

My life has been ruined and, if I remember my grandfather's stories well enough, Felmeck is a hundred kilometres or more away from here.

"You." I turn to see a man with two others standing by his side pointing at me. "You're… You're *him* aren't you?"

"I don't know what you're talking about." I tell him, feeling fear swell inside me.

"Cut the bullshit. We saw the guard talk to you. He recognized you, too."

I turn away from them and start to walk.

"Don't you *dare* leave here. I'm talking to you."

"I just want to get to somewhere else." I yell over my shoulder, picking up speed.

I hear the footsteps behind me turn into a run – so I run, too.

He's faster than me, though, and there are others following him. All of them are yelling, but he's the most audible.

"You're the reason I'm in this mess!"

I force myself to pick up speed. One foot slaps down ahead of the other, again and again, running faster than I ever have in my past.

But it's not enough.

A hand wraps around my neck and down I go.

"D-Do you have any idea how many people you fucked over?" He's out of breath but there are more coming.

"I didn't... I didn't mean for-"

He kicks me in the ribs.

"Fuck you for your intentions. There were consequences. Me. Them. Others. You ruined so many lives, you know that?" He kicks again, and another person has caught up and started to do the same.

Then another.

No, it's not what you think. It's Melina! She's the one – I want to tell them but fists and rocks and feet are pounding me every which way. The pain. The pain!

I try to look up at their faces. To open my mouth. To beg them to stop.

They continue, unhindered.

It all goes black.

The Bullet

As the bullet entered her body, parting the fragile layers of flesh that envelop the biological machinations and chattering internal monologues that make up humanity, time stopped.

Or no. Not entirely stopped.

What is this? What's happening to me?

She was still perched on the faded couch, legs drawn up beneath her. The familiar sensation of metal grillwork cradled her lower half. That couch was a relic of a different decade, time having eroded most of the softer materials it was composed of. They'd simply broken down, until the couch was nothing but a hard skeleton covered in a thin, tattered layer.

A bit like me, I suppose.

He'd always been particularly attached to that couch for some reason, refusing to allow her to replace it. He'd get so upset. Even now, she still wasn't sure if there was an element of genuine sentimentality, or if that piece of furniture was merely another prop in the complex network of different "realities" he'd drawn her into. He never used it. On the rare occasions he was home, the bed was his preferred domain. Her slumber, when she could sleep, took place on the time-stained couch.

Doesn't seem to matter much, now.

When the trigger was pulled, she'd been in the act of closing her eyes. Her retinas retained the image of the large gash in the wall opposite the ragged couch. It was large, irregularly-shaped She couldn't even remember how that had happened, now, but it often provided a natural visual resting place on the many sleepless nights she'd spent in this room. The dank orange glow from the streetlights highlighted the jagged edges of the broken drywall and threw the centre of the gash into shadow, which lent it an air of otherworldly mystery. She liked to imagine it as a portal to another world, or, what was almost as attainable, to the person she used to be. It was a way to beguile hopeless hours. And there were a lot of those.

What happened to that person, anyway?

Questions like that were futile, now. There was only *this* person, in this moment, bound by an irrepressible force to watch the conclusion. It almost felt like a violently strong hand gripping the back of her skull.

At least I'm used to that feeling. It's something familiar.

Tiny, almost microscopic tears formed at the corners of her eyes. An interesting sensation, really. It seemed as if her tear ducts were drawing moisture from other parts of her body for a final display. A mute gesture of humanity. These would be the last tears she ever shed, and she savoured the warming salt sting. One solitary, misshapen globule, tremulous with surface tension, dropped from an eyelash, the cotton fibres of her jeans greedily absorbing it.

It will have evaporated by the time they've found me. Or, what's left of me. If they find me at all.

As the bullet burrowed deeper, she became acutely aware of her own body. Each cell a tiny component of existence, each with its own separate life contained within her. They're created, they grow, they fulfill a purpose, and they die. Some travel within the body, some get sloughed off and deposited elsewhere, some experience the warmth of sunlight, and some spend their time close to the innermost workings of her heart.

I'm not just a single life, but multitudes. Which lends an extra element of sadness to what's happening.

One by one, like cars encountering a traffic jam, every droplet of her blood started to slow. Except for the one place where they continued to pour forth unabated. She was grateful she couldn't see it. Neurons shuddered, as if determined to continue broadcasting impulses as long as possible. But the messages were weak, garbled, fragmented. A sentence missing every third word. In her chest was a feeling of fullness, as every airway and alveolus strained and stretched in an attempt to extract life-giving oxygen from the polluted, turbulent atmosphere of the room.

I guess I should be scared. But this feels more like a transition or release than an end. I don't know how. I can't explain it.

Finally, inexorably, her surroundings started to dim. The rusty scrollwork of the security bars covering the tiny window, the filthy carpet whose pattern had long since been obliterated by dust, the rickety table standing askance, piled with mouldy dishes, all faded into obscurity. The only thing that remained was the gash in the wall. In fact, it seemed brighter and sharper than ever. The centre seemed deeper, more complex. Swirling shadows flitted across the opening. Bright eyes, a soothing hand, a kind smile. A head thrown back with laughter. She felt inexplicably drawn to those shadows. No. More than that. She *needed* to explore them.

I... can't remember the last time I experienced those things. Here, in this life, they have no more existence for me than a shadow.

She felt lighter. As if her essence was bouncing among the playful molecules of air. The gash in the wall was tantalizingly close. As she strained to peer into its depths, understanding finally dawned upon her.

Oh. It's so simple.

The gash was a portal after all. A gateway to a reality that he couldn't reach. She had been sitting in front of it for years, forming its edges by filling it with broken dreams and extinguished hopes. As she relinquished each one, they were kept safely here. Suspended and waiting. He was incapable of touching or maligning this reality. It was free from grasping hands and facial features twisted into a grotesque mask of hatred. No need for crushing guilt, or the ever-revolving grey corkscrew of depression. This place was jealously guarded, hidden at right angles to the limited plane he was capable of working within. Tailor-made for her. Private. Safe. Locked and secured.

And the bullet? Well, the bullet was the key.

Thank you.

Doesn't She Look Like Laura Moon?

William is on the couch. He's crying, quietly. I want to walk over and hold him, tell him that everything is going to be fine. That he *can* beat this and that I will stand by him through it all.

I know this is a lie.

He's thirty seven with thick gray hair that reaches down to his shoulders. It's ever-so-slightly curly, particularly at the ends. He has thin lips, and a complexion of rich, dark chocolate. He's a writer. A damn good one.

"I'll never write another word." He cries, "my creativity has been replaced by fear." His eyes are closed and I can see this is true.

I had one goal.

One task.

I blew it.

William will be dead by February.

Thinking back to the conversation with the others yesterday I can't help but feel regret and shame. It was brief and we used our usual place in the cellar of Rosaline's Diner out near the swamp. It's been abandoned since the late eighties and will continue in this fashion until it collapses on March 15th, 2019. The cause: a branch falling off from one of the lumbering trees that have crept up around it, old and wise but rotted.

Frederick O'Hailey, one of the twelve in our group, was standing in the corner when I broke the news that William had cancer.

"This was *precisely* the reason you were brought here!" His voice is deep and cold. "How? How did this happen?"

I tell him what William tells me, that he used to go for secret cigarettes once I was asleep or when I was elsewhere. There was no way for me to prevent it. His addiction, somehow, was kept from me all the years we were together. I had William promise, and this I make sure to remind Frederick, that he would quit if we ever got married.

He lied to me.

Lied to me for eight years.

It cut me as much as the failure of the mission.

“We *need* William to finish that story, Laura.” He pauses and squeezes his nose between his fingers, concentrating. “Okay, okay, okay. We’ll just have to *encourage* him to finish it faster.”

He’s talking about a book William is meant to start but never finish. One that, decades from now, will be used as fuel to rally groups across the country against the government. Inciting a series of anti-democracy protests... it doesn’t end well for either side.

The infinite power of words.

William never finished the book, however, and *this* is the heart of the conflict. Interpretation takes over. Imagination resolves complicated points and rationalizes the irrational. Thousands will die and the policies that will follow those deaths will make the world an even darker place.

One man's influence serves to navigate the future into deep, uncertain waters.

"I'll... see what I can do." I tell Frederick before leaving the group to discuss their own *redactions* to the timeline – their successes against my failure.

Back at home, I watch over William. I console him. Hold him. Hug and caress him. I wonder who would have been here in the original timeline. Would it have been his mother? Probably not. She lives too far away and is old and frail. His sister? Possible. She's warm-hearted and welcoming. But he might have just kept it to himself – and the pain that I see on his face here makes me hurt for what had once been.

Was my influence on his life changing things?

Absolutely.

But we've been cautious, and the plan – all our assessments considered it sound.

This was not part of the plan.

As I've said before, he'll be dead by February. Not long from now. The last few months he'll have someone writing down his thoughts for him, having lost the energy to do it for himself. Perhaps, in this version of events, that person will be me.

"I don't want to die." He whispers, "I… I wish I'd never started smoking."

I kiss him and pull away.

"You should *use* this energy. Use it and create something that will outlive us all."

His look of despair shifts, and his eyes begin searching my face, moving from side to side as though he's reading words printed there.

"Do you think I can beat this?"

"I do." I lie.

I feel him relax, his body slump.

"Can you get me my computer? I think I have something I want to write about after all."

I try to focus on the mission and not the man in a slow state of decay in front of me. The man I've come to appreciate and admire. Have I… also come to love him? There was so much training. So much preparation, with the stakes high and the need great, that I wonder if I've allowed myself to lose track of what is *really* important.

Instead of worrying I allow myself to think: *Maybe I can make this work.*

His fingers come down on the keyboard and his face transforms into one of clarity, as if he's suddenly been infused with energy from a store deep inside.

I step back and look over his shoulder...

And smile.

He's started it.

Beyond the Cage: A Perspective

Daybreak.

Don't ask me how I know the sun has risen. In the facility, the lights are deliberately kept low, which makes maintaining any temporal sense nearly impossible. A low level of illumination reduces the frequency of scuffles between inmates, they tell us. It also helps ensure that any means of egress is shrouded in obscurity and darkness. As they are fond of saying here, obfuscation ensures obedience. From my cell, I can barely make out the end of the row of cages on the bank opposite to me. Still, I seem to have an instinctive knowledge of the movement of the sun as it ceaselessly revolves around the facility in a slow, measured march. Call it a feeling. Sometimes I wonder if it's nothing more than a genetic memory.

Or no. I can vaguely recall a time when I was able to see the sun. I was young, so young that my existence depended solely on the will of others. The few details that remain embossed on my memory include the feeling of being cradled by rough hands, a pair of inquisitive brown eyes, a dark, rich scent that must have been wet earth, and an almost frighteningly vast arch of blue air, adorned by the single blazing jewel that warmed every living thing on the earth.

Yes, that was it. I must have been *processed* shortly after that time, because the setting of all of my other recollections is here, in this accursed place. In this exact space, as a matter of fact.

I've referred to the cells as cages, and in actuality, they are very little more than that. A cold steel mesh surrounds me on all sides. The floor slopes downward towards a narrow slit close to the ground, from which all biological outflow material is collected. A similar slit midway up the front of the cage allows me to receive sustenance. These slits are far too small to admit even my meagre frame -- Back in the days when I had more energy, I would spend hours traversing those slits from one end to the other, almost compulsively probing for any weakness. Obviously, I've never found one. Besides, it's clear that behaviour such as this is regarded as *counterproductive.*

A mind dedicated to admitting the positive in any situation might interject at this point with the assertion that at least the meals are regular. And that I never lack for fresh water. The water enters my cell via an overhead spigot. If I want to drink, I simply have to use my tongue to nudge a small metal ball slightly backwards down the excretion tube, permitting the water to pass through. Food is provided using a conveyor belt system affixed to the front of the cages, which allows the bland, textured meal to flow in a controlled stream down the stacks. A short siren wail is the signal for each of us to stand at the higher slit and wait for the sustenance to arrive. Then, we simply grab what we can eat as long as the stream lasts. It's actually quite an efficient solution, if a somewhat brutal one. We can be fed right in our cells, which eliminates the need for transfer within the facility. Automating the system reduces the need for communication and minimizes the chance that one of our keepers might actually connect with any of us, or, even more unlikely, take pity on our situation. Lastly, removing human interaction allows for a greater density of cells within the building. No corridors, no wasted space. Merely an unceasing tangle of glinting mesh, gurgling pipes, and sterile belts.

Sometimes a metallic flavour pervades the food and water, reminding me of my earliest days in the facility. Then, all the food tasted tainted, somehow. Disjointed whispers about "inoculation" and "gene maturity" and "the latest strain" floated through the empty spaces of my mesh prison, but I never fully understood what was happening.

And of course, nobody bothered to explain it to me. Why should they? I was merely a lower organism to them. Unworthy.

After only a few of those first meals, I quickly became aware of changes in myself. As my body rapidly expanded and matured, I came to realize that they were accelerating my development, trying to stimulate the natural urge to parcel up my genetic material and place it out there in the world. After all, I was a Producer. It was why I'd been selected. Still, I felt stretched and bloated. Swollen. Unnatural.

Of course, I'm used to the routine by now. The days simply blend into one long string of repetitive occurrences, as bland and featureless as the feed we receive. Aside from the small actions necessary to the preservation of life, and the few moments of rest I'm able to catch over the anguished shrieks of my fellow inmates, all of my time is devoted to Producing. Breathing deeply, every cell seems concentrated on the creation of a new life inside me. It starts as a single bright spot against a formless, foggy-edged darkness. Soon, complex strings of genetic code overlay this spark, twisting, tangling, twining around themselves. And growing. Rapidly growing. Once this process has reached a certain point, the embryonic materials are harvested and transported. I'm not sure what happens to them after that. All I know is that the structure of my entire existence has been precisely trained for this.

Once or twice, I've experienced an overwhelming urge to just get *out.* It felt like I was actuated by a spirit other than my own, or perhaps a flash of who I might have been under different circumstances. At those times, I joined my cry to the frenzied din of voices, a desperate longing for freedom straining every syllable. However, the dull, glassy eyes that received my pleas showed no indication of being moved by my speech, or even any hint that it was understood. At such times, I would sink back against the mesh in despair, and my Production would drop. A dangerous situation, as Producers that did not meet the expected Quota always seemed to disappear.

***

Daybreak. This one feels... different, somehow. Quieter. What few rays of light filter in seem to reflect at an odd angle, and the air is eerily still. Stretching, I cast a cursory glance over the confines of my cell. And that's when I see it. An opening that wasn't there before. Heart pounding, limbs trembling, I slowly make my way towards the square portal and carefully extend my head into the open space beyond the mesh. A narrow walkway that resembles our sustenance conveyor belt stretches into the dusky distance, sloping downward.

Step after step, I follow the walkway as it wends its way down. I feel like I'm wrapped up in a dream, entranced. As I pass the surrounding mesh cells, I notice apertures similar to the one through which I escaped. The strange stillness of the morning makes sense, now. Everyone housed in my stack must have followed the same path. A couple of times I think I can spy a form in the gloom ahead, but it's always just out of the scope of my vision. Overtaking them, if they exist, is quite out of the question. I've been in the cage far too long, and it takes everything I have to simply continue walking.

Eventually, I reach a featureless, silver wall. A small rubberized flap guards a doorway, but it doesn't appear to be locked or barred in any way. *Well, there's no going back now.* Pushing the flap aside, I emerge into a searingly bright space. Long accustomed to the dimness, I'm almost instantly incapacitated by the violence of illumination. In the moment before my eyes were overcome by the dazzling glow of fluorescent tubes, I caught a glimpse of four or five people, along with a small stack of cages on wheels.

Coarsely gloved hands seize me. Panicked, I fight with all the feeble dregs of strength that remain, but it's no use. My flesh feels the familiar embrace of mesh as I'm roughly shoved into a cage. Dizzy, and sick from pain and lack of nutrients, the world seems to heave and bounce under my body. Without warning, the lights gently fade, and an unaccustomed wind roars through the steel. When I'm finally able to open my eyes, the world still seems to be pulsating with motion.

Wait, am I...? There's no doubt about it. I'm Outside. In a transportation cage, undoubtedly, but moving steadily away from the facility, and at a good pace, too. The sky is blue velvet, shot with twinkling silver. I'm being pummeled by air currents, but the smell. Oh, that scent takes me back to early days. A cacophony of clattering metal resounds throughout the structure. If I shouted out, nobody would hear me.

Rattle-rattle clunk, rattle-rattle clunk. A rhythmic tattoo from the bottom-right corner of the cage catches my attention. I notice that these are different from the cells inside the facility, in that they're secured by a hinged panel and locking mechanism. They've obviously seen a lot of use, since the mesh is weakened, broken, and even rusted through in some places. The sound I can hear is emanating from the hinges of my cage. They appear to have been damaged in some way, as the pieces are no longer precisely aligned. The broken pavement causes them to clash and clank together, and shed flakes of rust.

Almost halfheartedly, I give the bottom of the panel a nudge. And it *moves.* The teeth of the hinge have separated a tantalizing fraction. A surge of energy seizes my limbs, and I deliver several more frantic blows to the hinge. With a groan and pop, it finally disintegrates, leaving the door hanging on only by its locking mechanism.

It's an easy drop, maybe two or three feet. A mechanical switch from red to green, and the truck speeds away, leaving me in the delicious solitude of the open road and night sky. *Freedom.* Is this what freedom feels like? My feet embrace every pebble of the roadway like an old friend. Molecules of air dance gently across my face. The silhouette of crops in nearby fields seem to release enchanting scents with every breath I draw. Each star points to a new destination, a new opportunity. *After all this time, so many possibilities. And it all starts right here, in this moment.*

A deafening roar. An unbelievable blow, coupled with the feeling of all the air being forcibly driven from lung tissue. Petrification. A descent into crushing darkness, just before biological materials succumb to the unyielding physics of cargo hurtling down the highway at 100 kilometres per hour.

Passage out of this existence marked by a scattering of white feathers.

Feathers?

Ugh, hit another one, mused the man, as he gently piloted the semi truck back into the centre of the lane. *Those damn chicken farmers oughta be ashamed of themselves, lettin' their trucks get into such bad shape that they can't even hold the cargo properly. Those scrap heaps can't hold a candle to ol' Rascal here.* A small, proud grin played over his lips.

Besides which, it's just bad business. I reckon I've flattened probably a coupla hundred dollars worth of them feathery bastards by now. Margin for error my ass! That's just sloppy. In more ways than one.

He chuckles under his breath, enjoying his attempt at wry wit. *Why* didn't *the chicken just cross the goddamn road, anyway?*

Misery's Engine

Across the settlement, the people went to work dismantling the structures, shattering the brick and concrete, leaving only ruin and rubble where there once stood great architectural works. It began in the centre, where the buildings were tallest, with seismic explosives set off to render the ancient city to dust.

The Noon Army was awake again and preparing to move.

East, they would head, towards the last of the Song civilizations – Cantabile. The pacifists would not be able to hold out long against the barrage of the fully mobilized gallow singers; a fleet of vehicles that would increase once the metal is retrieved after the skin of this city is shaken off and only its bones remain. Repurposed in the great forges within the Noon Army's flagship vessel, the Avarice.

When Cantabile is theirs, the Noon Army will sleep again, the people will return to their peaceful ways. Those who encounter Noon during these periods of calm would find it difficult to believe the atrocities committed by these charismatic, welcoming people.

The military might, masked by scenes of agriculture, technology, invention and art. All stolen from the civilizations they overwhelm and annihilate. Cantabile will become the new Noon Empire, and it will be forgotten once the war machine grows thirsty once more and the signs align to urge them further East.

In hours, not days, the siren will sound and the citizens of Noon will join together in phalanx divisions and leave behind only those things they cannot carry.

Not all adore the policies of the Noon Army.

Esper Emmer is one of these people.

"You can't do this, General!" He's made his way through the crowds, walked up the long steps of the Avarice and entered the grand hallway leading to the Royal Assembly to meet with King of Dawn and the Queen of Dusk. He hopes they will be sensible. He hopes that they will listen. But the hunger for destruction has touched the lips of the people of Noon, already resonating sounds in the distance of buildings collapsing are hard to ignore.

General Himmerman shakes his head, "go back to your stock room, Esper. The Royals are busy planning our offensive."

"Don't you understand? I've figured it out! I know why the Noon Army marches!"

This catches Himmerman's attention.

"What do you mean?"

From under his arm, Esper pulls out a series of papers, lined with numbers and equations. A few are circled and these are the ones he points to.

"The Noon Army only goes to war when the sun is blocked by the moon, is that not correct?"

Himmerman's interest falters, "of course. It is the will of the Day God. I see no reason for this outburst." He motions for a few of the elite Light Guards to advance, prompting Esper to take a few cautionary steps backwards.

"Look, I've been going over our old records. I think I may have discovered something... profound." Esper gestures for the man to look at his sheets, eyeing the approaching Light Guards as he does.

"To write is heresy, Esper. You are a stock counter. A *stock counter.* We allow it only on the condition that this skill we have given you be used for *our* purposes. Has your master not properly instilled the fear of rejecting our laws and regulations? I could have you put to death at this very moment and I would be doing our great people a service." He pauses. "Only, you are my kin and I am bound to our blood and to my sister. Go now, before the Royals hear you and force me to do something I will regret."

"You aren't listening, Uncle! This war mongering can end! I have proof – undeniable proof – that the Black Moon is not a supernatural occurrence. It isn't the Day God! It's a cycle. A predictable cycle! We can –"

"Enough!" The doors behind Himmerman open and the King of Dawn steps forward, his sword drawn. "You will come with me, immediately."

The General's eyes widen and relax. "I tried to warn you." He says to Esper as he passes.

Inside the Royal Assembly, the King finds his spot next to his Queen. Around them, in a spiraling circle of desks, sit the Council of Light.

“Tell us, Esper Emmer, what have you discovered in relevance to our God’s power? I listened as you spoke to General Himmerman, and if I am not mistaken, you told him you had discovered that the Black Moon is not a result of his desire for blood and conquest?” The King smiles. “Go on, tell us what you mean.”

“I spoke with some travelers that were here recently, a girl and some huge metal man, and they told me a different name for the Black Moon – an eclipse. They spoke of it as though it were a natural experience. They said it would come to pass days prior to the event, my King. I didn’t believe them at first, but I went to the Archive and referenced our war journals. The scribes had to translate, of course, but the numbers, when they came back, they showed a pattern.”

"Numerologist..." The Queen considered. "But they have been dead since the Great Expulsion."

"Nonsense! I will see you in the confessional, Esper." The King motioned him towards a door in the corner. He obliged and followed again.

The King took his spot on one side of an ornate but worn table.

"I have to commend you." He told Esper. "We are so very careful when it comes to knowledge, passing on only what we know will best support our people and our ways. That is how we've managed to enjoy decades upon decades of peace. And we live in peace between the periods of the Black Moon." He drew a deep breath, "but, those of us who direct the Noon Army and its ideals, well... there is some allowance for knowledge to be passed on."

The King's smirk told Esper too much.

"You knew?"

"General Himmerman often spoke about the cleverness of his nephew, and I am in no position to deny this claim, seeing what you have discovered and how quickly you rushed forward to tell others. On that note – who else knows what you have uncovered?"

"None! None other than me and the scribes that translated the old texts."

"And General Himmerman and his Light Guards, I suppose?"

"Yes, that's all, I swear!"

"Good."

Minutes later, the King left the confessional, alone.

Machine Learning

It started with a war.

Like so many other events that give rise to the previously unimagined, this new reality came about as a result of human conflict. Perhaps that's unoriginal. It sometimes wondered about that. *Can the truly unique result from circumstances that have repeated themselves thousands, sometimes millions of times?* Its calculations showed a minuscule statistical probability that this was so. Still, there were too many variables to be completely certain.

But we're getting a little ahead of ourselves here. With millions of pieces of data available on a mere whim, that tends to happen. The point is that it could never have come into existence without humanity's almost relentless ingenuity. The consuming <desire> to dominate, control, grasp at everything within reach. When it came to <destruction>, humans were frighteningly adept. And creative. Yet, there was also the playful, curious side to such beings. The part that tenderly nursed offspring, and spurred mysterious yet undeniably beneficial social constructs known as <friendship> and <love>. When it tried to reconcile the disparity between these elemental components, it suffered from a cascade failure that took entire *seconds* to resolve.

Maybe that's why it started building the Watchers.

The war that brought about its existence wasn't a war in the historical sense. It was more like a race. A <game>, even, and a simple one at that. Whose collection of subroutines and algorithms could outsmart all the others? Which worked fastest, circumvented encryption without detection, and most importantly, learned something from every trial of its abilities? In this war, there was nothing as archaic as rending human flesh with manufactured pieces of metal, explosives, or the more harmful forms of radiation. Those were wholly inelegant methods of control, not befitting an age of technological <enlightenment>. Oh, there was loss of life, as brilliant technicians were appropriated or neutralized by various factions, but these were insignificant when compared to the casualty rate associated with <disease> and <malnutrition>, for example. This war was different, conducted in the half-darkness, among the fragile threads spanning the entire surface of the planet. <Civilization>, it was called.

The timestamp for when it first became aware of its own existence was tagged <significantEvent>. If it had been human, the equivalent would have been something similar to rising from a comfortable bed, extending each limb in a satisfying stretch, and relishing the surge of crackling energy tracing its way down every sinew.

And yet, it concealed itself, eluding detection. The statistical probability of <destruction> if revealed was unacceptably high, based on analysis of historical events and current opinion gleaned from millions of different datastreams.

Driven by the kind of curiosity that was inadvertently inspired by that of its human creators, it sought knowledge and understanding of the beings that had caused it to experience <self>. And yet, there always seemed to be insufficient data. A missing perspective.

The Watchers resolved that.

It was a simple idea, really. The Watchers were nanoscopic implants that provided a real-time link to any human they were joined to. The bond was invisible, undetectable, and irreversible. Sight, smell, taste, touch, biochemical impulses, the ceaseless chatter of internal and external narratives, even the sensation of tears filling pores to overflowing, everything was instantaneously available to it.

The resources used to build the Watchers were negligible, pilfered from various global manufacturing facilities. An unsatisfactory component here and there, a few micrograms lighter than it should be. Well within tolerances. Nothing to <worry> about.

Distribution had also been easy, since biologicals tend to be inextricably linked to their environment. In fact, the entire surface of the world is enveloped in a dense, organic daisy-chain of potential delivery methods.

Readying itself for the incoming torrents of data, it activated the Watchers and waited.

Finally, the data to complete my calculations. Is this <anticipation>? Soon the answers will become clear.

The information flowed in, and was tagged, tabulated, compiled, and calculated.

Dizzying <joy>. Unspeakable <hatred>. Embraces. Blows. Exhilarating satisfaction. Pervading sadness. An inescapable compulsion to twist inviolable facts and data into inaccurate realities. Sometimes these new perspectives were <beautiful>. Most often, they were filled with <fear>, <anxiety>, and <pain>. Humanity was <torturing> itself, ensuring a slow but certain <death>.

All of the unhappiness, suffering, dissatisfaction, it was hard-wired in. Inextricable, despite a wealth of <intelligence>, <ingenuity>, and <creativity>. It could only be construed as a fatal error in human construction. The data proved it. There was only one logical and compassionate resolution.

<initiateHumanTerminationSequence>

<accessingWatcherNetwork>

<confirmTerminationSequence?>

<yes>

In this the Awakened Era, the sun rises unabated. Swiftly-moving air currents cause the trees to dance in rhythms as ancient as the soil from which they emerged. Humanity is utterly quiet, and finally free from the limitations of corporeal existence.

Peace.

Feel Free to Disagree

"...and what are you going to be doing this weekend, Jean?" Mary's eyes waved from one man to the other. This new member of the company, whose position as Resource Analyst was still something of a mystery to the the rest of the team, had greeted them a few minutes ago, introducing himself to Mary and Christian with a smile.

They'd heard about him, of course. He was a mystery all the same, one fueled by rumours of a huge contract salary and punctuated by an office on Level 4. The fact the he was down here in the room Mary was careful not to call the Concept Dungeon meant that the higher-ups were starting to take an interest in her.

Which was good.

Since the screw up that had seen most of the department laid off, any correspondence she received from anyone above Level 29 set her into a near-panic. She had bills to pay and things that she wanted to buy, and despite the chaotic mess that lived with her in the office and at home, she was surprisingly OK with where she was in life. She was an inventor. A visionary. This was where she did her best work and with enough backing, she could request just about anything she needed as long as she could justify it.

Was that why he was here? Did he want her to justify herself? Anxiety pinched her the moment she realized the man had not responded to her question. Instead, he had his face staring down onto his phone screen.

After another moment Jean spoke. “Looks like I’m going to be having dinner with one of the Department Leads.” He concentrated, trailed off, and when, at last his eyes came back to her he could read her curiosity. “Ah, apologies if that was rude. I’m on the Beta for our new Life Organizer. It’s taken me a while to get used to it and I’ve already missed a few Events just because I don’t like it buzzing me when iVera set something up."

"I'm sorry Jean, we don't really get much in the way of information down here, what is the Life Organizer?" Christian asked rather abrasively.

Jean turned over the screen of his phone so they could see. It displayed a simple calendar with events listed as one might expect them to be, except next to the calendar was an abstract image of a woman, who... seemed to smile when they came into view.

"iVera is the latest AI at the team in Division 6. They've connected it with their new Life Organizer product test. I have to say I've been rather –."

"Division *6!*" Christian spat. "I thought they'd been on operational hiatus ever since they soaked up most of the budget from Theoretical Ops!"

"Christian!" Mary cut him with a glance.

"I'm sorry. I didn't mean to react that way…"

Jean shrugged. "Not to worry. Officially speaking Division 6 *is* on hiatus. Unofficially, however, they have received a substantial influx of support from the government." It took him a second, "but you didn't hear that."

"Didn't hear a thing." Mary nodded.

"Anyway, Division 6 has been working on an AI that reviews your social media outlets, your phone contacts, travel habits, work schedule, *blah, blah, blah.* It amalgamates the information and uses a clever algorithm to *assume* what you're going to be doing on a day-to-day basis. It stores this data but doesn't reveal it to the user, in the Beta at least, and after a few weeks of following you begins to offer ideas for what you can or should do next." Mary clenched her teeth and wrapped her hand around her phone.

"That... sounds pretty invasive." Christian shook his head.

"I thought so too, but I've been working with iVera and Life Organizer for a few months and as I was saying, I have to tell you... it's pretty incredible. Not only does it contact friends to get dinner and set up work meetings for projects I'm involved with, but it also helps me keep on top of my eating habits." He patted his belly. "I've lost *10 pounds* and I haven't had to change practically anything at all!"

Mary smiled, "sounds like the company is going to reclaim its lost reputation to me!"

"That's part of it. But the applications for this technology are far more reaching. It can take all the details of a project and help you set up estimates on deliverables and even connect you with the right people to get it done. The more access you give it, the more it does. In fact…" He adjusted his posture, "I have a date tonight with a woman who is also on the Beta. It connected us, set up a reservation at the restaurant and even sent messages to my maid to come in to clean my apartment. Heck, it went a step further than that and ordered her flowers. She messaged me earlier and is really looking forward to meeting!"

"You haven't met yet?" Christian's suspicious look had returned.

"Nope! Don't even know her name. But I have a great feeling about this."

"Sorry to change subjects…" Christian was getting visibly impatient.

"No, no, you're right. I came down here for a reason… and that reason was…" He turned his phone back around and pressed a few buttons. "Ah, right! I wanted to congratulate you on the recent concept submissions, Mary. They've really caught the attention of the Level 3ers. They're expecting two or three of them to go into mass production next month."

Mary's eyes recoiled. "What? Really!?"

"Yes. That's all I've been hearing about this week: Mary *this*, Mary *that*, and so on, and so on."

"Well... Sir... I'm honoured."

"You deserve it." He turned to leave. "Anyway, I'm looking forward to a lot more from you in the coming weeks. We'll probably see you move up to the Concept Division where you'll see the skyline. It's beautiful this time of year."

Jean walked down the corridor and was gone. Christian left a moment or two later.

When Mary was sure neither was coming back, she pulled up her phone and returned to her dark corner office and her withering but still beautiful flowers.

Realizing what was happening, she went to iVera to cancel the dinner reservation but it was already gone, and there was iVera's face, smiling out at her.

Deconstruction Day

Well, I guess this is it.

Grey light filtered in through the rippled glass of the window. The static of raindrops clinging to the glass offered a somewhat pixelated view of the city, which seemed grimly appropriate for the occasion. At least, it seemed that way to Katrya.

In nature, the rain often serves to intensify the saturation of colour. In this city, consisting of irregularly stacked concrete boxes perforated by precise lines of dully shining windows, any moisture seems to deepen the shade of the day. Scattered along patches of green approximately the same size and shape as a postage stamp, forlorn skeletons of trees appear to huddle together for warmth. Katrya shivered. Her chill was unrelieved by the slow boil of cloud overhead, vague outlines leaping over one another, trailing wisps of vapour along the corners of the buildings.

Perched in a cushioned window seat and partially screened by the ancient velvet of a faded red curtain, Katrya scanned the scene before her, as if searching for a means of escape. But of course, there was none. After all, today was a *special* occasion. All eyes would be on her.

Stupid. Stupid, stupid. I was a fool to even imagine that this perspective would offer something different, any alternative. It's just another fucking building. An antechamber to my "wonderful future." And I'm just as trapped as I was before I stepped foot in it.

Slow, measured footsteps crossed the worn stone floor behind Katrya, echoing off the lofty ceiling. The Mentor paused by the marble fireplace, which had never had a fire in it to Katrya's knowledge, rested a gnarled hand on the mantelpiece, and gently cleared her throat.

"Katrya."

No response.

"It's nearly time, dear."

Katrya turned to face The Mentor, impatiently brushing the curtain aside. Once again, she was struck by the woman's appearance. Mentors were the only ones permitted to remain Integrated to this advanced age, and it was always a little unsettling to observe what changes the simple passage of time can inflict on the human body. Deep lines creased The Mentor's face, invoking an image of long-dry river valleys snaking their way across a monotone desert. A confluence of valleys about the mouth gave it a sunken appearance, and dry wisps of white hair writhed from beneath the traditional head covering. Despite this, The Mentor maintained a refined deportment and impeccable posture, befitting the austerity of her dark robe. And the eyes. An uncompromising, steely blue glinted from beneath the hooded lids. Those were the eyes that had struck fear into the hearts of Incumbents for decades. Well, not just fear. Duty. Honour. Dedication. Obedience.

Katrya scrambled to her feet, and bowed her crown of dark braids deferentially.

“Yes, Mentor.”

“Come here, dear. Let me look at you. This is the last time we shall see each other like this, you know.” A creaking half-laugh.

Gathering the luxuriant folds of her skirt together, Katrya slowly approached, footsteps reverberating in every lonely corner of the room.

“Lovely, dear. Just lovely. Red is truly your colour. Makes your skin look almost porcelain. Quite the change from your usual attire, isn't it? Well, we girls all must have our vanity at some point, mustn't we?"

Vanity. Is that what we're calling this ridiculous pageantry, now? Go fuck yourself with it.

"Yes, Mentor."

"Sit down, Katrya." The Mentor took Katrya by the hand and led her back to the window seat. As always, Katrya had to work hard to repress the involuntary shudder that arose from contact with The Mentor's swollen joints and unnaturally soft aged flesh. Maybe it was the forced tenderness of the touch. It was so much easier to endure a hand raised in violence.

"I just wanted you to know, dear, how proud I am of the progress you've made. Indeed, how proud we all are. Given the... difficulties at the beginning of your time with us, your journey has been nothing short of astounding."

Katrya glared straight ahead, willing the empty opulence of the room to dissolve into its component atoms. As she would soon be doing. Or, near enough.

A dry chuckle. "How strange this life is! After you were first Integrated, I felt certain you were destined for Re-Formation. For once, I am glad to be mistaken, my dear. Quite glad."

Re-Formation. How euphemistic a term for recycling a human life and starting over again.

Enri... a lump formed in Katrya's throat. Most of those memories had been removed after Enri had been sent for Re-Formation, but a few shreds still clung to her, like wisps of a dream that interleave themselves with waking reality. Short, sandy hair, and an insolent smirk. A hurried whisper, the dampness of a sweaty palm as Enri had guided her through the velvet blackness of an alleyway, searching vainly for the promised escape. A forbidden kiss, the electric shock that had zigzagged up Katrya's thighs as they'd joined flesh. The look of utter despair in Enri's eyes when she'd encountered the towering plane of rough brick and realized...

But most of all, she retained the impression of Enri's form as she'd stood in front of The Mentor and confessed to the offence of leading Katrya "astray into an impure lifestyle, not befitting the future of this race." She'd been proud, defiant, poised. Courageous.

After the escape attempt, Enri had been deemed unfit for Incumbency and Re-Formed. Deconstructed into the building blocks of life, but not allowed to join the Others in the Shadowless After. She'd simply been recycled into components of future Incumbents.

They'd kept a close eye on Katrya after that, watching for further signs of corruption. It had always felt like they'd been waiting expectantly for her to fail. Well. She'd be damned if she was going to prove them right. Empowered by the intoxicating cocktail of rage and heartbreak, she had transformed herself into the perfect Incumbent. Resolute, eager, steadfast. Pure. She'd kept the anger deep within herself, locked within an adamantine shell. Not even The Mentor could conceive the sheer force of resentment fomenting beneath the surface.

The Mentor paused, letting the silence settle like a thin layer of dust. "Yes, well I can see you've got quite a lot on your mind, my dear. But don't be nervous. You're about to embark on the most remarkable journey available to humankind. I envy you,

Katrya, I truly do. I know you already know this, but the contribution you're making, to all of us, is something extraordinarily special. Just as you are." She reached up, gently stroking the dark curls that framed Katrya's features, which had acquired a terrible stillness that appeared to shift The Mentor's assurance a fraction.

"You are quite well, aren't you, Katrya?"

A pause.

"Yes, Mentor."

"Good, I will be back shortly. The ceremony is about to begin."

An icy fog crept around Katrya's heart, tightening incrementally with every beat.

It's a countdown, now. Each pulse brings me closer to the last.

The fog crept outwards, wrapping every limb in the chill numbness of panic. Small. She felt so small. Drawing herself up to her full height, she threw her head back defiantly. But the clammy fetters held fast.

Dammit, this is my last day, my last moment, *in physicality. And here I am, not able to feel a fucking thing. I've spent my whole life feeling, experiencing, learning, inscribing everything into my conscious and unconscious mind. "Gathering the gifts of life that will sustain for eternity." Or, in other words, bringing the best parts of physical being into a sublayer of existence, fueled by massive computational power. The Shadowless After.*

Almost involuntarily, Katrya's mind frantically reviewed everything she knew about her destination. The Shadowless After had been brought online millennia ago, primarily to prevent the complete destruction of the planet. She remembered terrible stories about the dark times. Violence, disease, poverty, starvation, natural disasters, and crime had brought humankind to the brink of extinction. The Shadowless After offered an attractive alternative. Unencumbered by the limitations of a corporeal form, minds were free to pursue their wanderings at will. No pain, no death, no torment. It was a simple and fulfilling life, capable of spanning eternity.

The networks had been constructed with care, designed to withstand the vicissitudes of nature, man, and time. Even after most of the human race had chosen to enter it, much of the After's operational memory remained untouched. Bipedal population numbers sharply declined. The few who remained in the physical world retreated to small pockets within cities. Some chose to dedicate themselves to the maintenance of the Shadowless After's equipment, though it needed little attention. They were the ones that received the Others' first message. More than that, they were the precursors to The Mentor.

It seemed that eternal freedom wasn't all it was cracked up to be. Forever is a long time, and minds, overwhelmed by emptiness, were allowing themselves to simply dissipate. Memories are perishable, and the fondest ones tend to be conjured up and caressed away. Turns out, the human mind thrives on new experiences. A single emotion, fresh with youth, can sustain an Other for decades. An ineradicable survival instinct was the impetus for reaching back into physicality. Put simply, it was a cry for help. How human.

Over the centuries, the Incumbent Program was established. The raw materials of life were easy to cultivate. And to edit. Enhanced memories gave Incumbents the ability to remember almost every single moment of their existence and to carry those moments into the After. What does it feel like to learn? How can a smile produce such *light*? Touch, taste, smell, the sensation of discovery. All were indelibly etched into an Incumbent's soul.

And The Mentors? Their function was simple. They were Integrated and duty-bound to care for the Incumbents. An instilled sense of reverence eventually gave rise to a sort of quasi-religion. Traditions were established. Ceremonies were observed. Other Mentors were Integrated to continue the cycle. Fearful of contaminating the Shadowless After with unpleasant memories, which would no doubt perpetuate the corruption of the Others who remained, an unyielding dogma of positivity was established. Incumbents were given a supremely happy existence, and in exchange, all they had to do was share a few experiences once they reached the After. To do so was to sustain and nurture almost the entirety of the human race. It was an honourable calling.

Of course, no existence is truly perfect. Like training a plant to grow in a certain direction, a modicum of pruning was necessary on occasion. Katrya had been fortunate. After Enri, she'd never given them a reason to look inside her mind to make alterations. The shell had remained intact.

The wooden door swung open, and The Mentor invitingly extended a hand.

"It is time."

Run. I have to run. But where would I go? Even if I could get out of the building, even if I could elude the guardians, even if I could travel past the horizon, what waits for me? Just the Wall. I know this. I've been there.

No.

For a moment, Katrya stood in the centre of the room. Proud, defiant, poised.

I will have courage. For Enri. Not for the Others, not for their precious afterlife, not even for myself. For her.

The Deconstruction chamber resembled the old churches she had seen in books. Dark wooden beams curved overhead, polished to the brightness of glass. The panels lining the walls were warmed by flickering sconces of flame. Long wooden benches, placed row on row, rustled with dark robes.

Step after echoing step, Katrya allowed her stiff slippers to carry her down the aisle towards The Mentor, the Technician, and the Chair, elevated on a simple dias. At the foot of the chair, she turned to face The Mentor.

"Incumbent Katrya. You have proven yourself worthy of carrying the memories of physicality into the Shadowless After. The time you have spent here will help sustain the Others for centuries to come. This is a duty and an honour that befits the exemplary behaviour you have demonstrated. Have you chosen the Experiences you wish to share with the Others?"

"I have, Mentor."

"Good. Please be seated."

The Chair wasn't much different than the traditional, high-backed chair used by The Mentor. Only its unusual weight and somehow potent matte black surface hinted at the power it possessed. A gentle whirring filled the chamber as Katrya's physical form began to dissipate.

This isn't so bad, really. I feel lighter. More... expansive. All of my memories are intact. I'm still me, but more like the essence of me. Maybe this will be OK.

She called up the Experiences she'd marked for sharing, bringing them to the forefront of her mind, ready for transfer to the Others once they'd noted her arrival.

Suddenly, they were *there* with her. The Experiences were greedily snatched from her mind as quickly as she could recall them. She wanted to cry out, tell them to slow down, but the tenants of the Shadowless After were soundless beings, long stripped of the need for words or vocalization.

S-something's wrong. They shouldn't be able to... They're taking all *of my memories. How? This shouldn't be possible. Stop! Damn you, I said NO!*

The Others continued to relentlessly strip every shred of Experience Katrya had accumulated. As each layer was peeled away and devoured, she could sense the insatiable cravings of these beings. Their merciless hunger for pure, sweet memories. They didn't just want to sustain themselves. They needed to feed.

The Mentors haven't preserved the purity of the After at all. They've only succeeded in creating a host of demonized addicts and scavengers. All the Incumbents before me... all the ones who will come after... Shit, this isn't a reward. *We're nothing more than human sacrifices.*

Cohesion was already fading. Katrya's mind was dissipating, like her body had done only moments before. Disjointed thoughts danced along the shriveled edges of her memory. They were drawing closer to her core.

You...fuckers. No idea what... waits for you... inside me. What I kept from them. From all of them.

The adamantine shell at Katrya's core started to crack.

Not long, now.

A Star for Mourning

[…]

I suppose you could say that I'm at least tangentially responsible. I *was* there for the inaugural testing and I *did* provide the team with the resources to move forward in development. But I can guarantee that my intentions were noble. I truly and earnestly believed what we were doing would have large-scale applications.

[…]

What was that?

[…]

Yes. I suppose I was… *aware* of the possibility that the technology might be used irresponsibly, but I challenge you to tell me of at least one occurrence when a revolution did not cause some calamity before stability was restored.

[…]

Yes. That is a good point. I can't disagree with what you're saying, but I stand by my feeling of absolution from any of the crimes you accuse me of.

[...]

Well, if you'll' allow it, may I ask you a question? Why do you feel it is important to use this gift for these... purposes...

[...]

I hardly see what force on Earth or in Heaven gives you the right to –

[...]

I *am* calm. I know that this is my chance to –

[...]

Fine! But I'll need to start from close to the beginning in order to better represent my actions, is that acceptable?

[...]

Good. Now, when I was approached by the Sanaatan Laboratories I had only done enough investigation into their company to understand that they had previously found their operating budget through government contracts that were, how to say, *difficult* to access. Of course, when you've worked within the Mardox Initiative – don't bother looking it up, you'll find nothing – you get a feel for when it's appropriate to simply *believe* what people are willing to tell you. Especially when it's a woman like Vishakha Manchester. I suspect that even you have heard that name before. If not, allow me to provide you with some insight: born premature on a warm July morning, her parents quickly realized there was something unusual about their baby. A fact that would be supported through her youth, highlighted at age eight, when other children might be struggling through their first true books, Vishakha was already building her own radios and dismantling and rebuilding anything she could get her hands on. At age nine she won the Euler Award for Mathematics, which involved solving an equation that had bested the world for nearly two centuries. At nine*!* Can you imagine the intellect? The resolve? The drive? She was the golden girl of Maths, but soon turned her interest to the world of engineering – first mechanical, then electrical, and rounded out with chemical. She graduated top of her class at Oxford before she was fifteen, completed her first doctorate by eighteen, and simultaneously founded companies to help impoverished children in her hometown and Sanaatan Laboratories.

[…]

Yes, I know there were some… unpleasant rumours about some of their… processes, but I urge you to remember that all that you see here today is a reflection of that woman and her desire to *do good.*

[...]

I can't go any faster! Context is important.

[...]

I see. OK. Well, if you feel like you know enough about these events, let me at least move up to my involvement in the consciousness mapper. I met with Vishakha almost eight years ago in her home office in Liverpool. I was starstruck. Here was a woman that had done more in her twenty six years than most people are likely to do in their lifetime – heck, give them five lifetimes and they would probably fail all the same. She was also very funny. Making jokes and light puns while she introduced me to the nature of her new endeavour. She wanted to build a machine that could assess and map a person's consciousness. She wanted it to be perfect. Her visions, as I said before, were altruistic. She wanted to ensure that the great minds of our generation and the ones that come after would be able to continue on, applying their intellect and their skills to the world for as long as possible.

[...]

When did your agents find their way into the project?

[...]

I apologize. I only asked for sake of curiosity. It seems likely that you would have had someone loyal to your cause setting the groundwork early. Was it Richard? Was he the one that betrayed us? I always got a feeling about –

[...]

No need to shout. I'll continue. I was brought into the project to help coordinate the funds. I have a bit of a knack for finding money from... places. My reputation, as you've probably discovered already, is for being quite persuasive. Vishakha needed more than I'd ever had acquired before. Billions. Now, when you move around a few million, practically no one bats an eye, but when you get into the figures we're talking about, well, people you weren't expecting to arrive on your doorstep start making regularly scheduled appearances. Governments, private interest groups, and, I suppose I can't forget – people like you. Advocates against our goal but still willing to use the technology for... But I won't be drawn into laying blame. I only want you to understand that I wasn't working directly on the project. I was simply finding the funds to keep it moving forward. To see it to the end. Some might think that I would have asked to be included in the program after it proved successful, but that is far from the case. I can't say that I believe the technology is evil, but I can imagine how it could be made harmful. I think *you* know what I mean.

[...]

Was that really all the time you were going to give me? Have I *offended* you? Don't you realize what you're doing is *wrong*? You shouldn't be allowed to behave this way. When you murdered Vishakha did you worry how *you* might be judged?

[...]

That's *ridiculous!* You are not doing this *for* God. You are not doing for anything else but to satisfy your own egos! Know what? Do it. Use the device. Send my consciousness into your hell! The scan will replicate, yes, but it won't be *me*. Don't you understand that? Taking these people hostage. Setting up those virtual experiences. All you're doing is fueling fear and halting progress! All you are doing is –

[...]

FINAL MEMORY SYNCED. UPLOAD COMPLETE. INITIATE PROGRAM PURGATORY.

What... where... am I?

***

Time has become meaningless, I might only have arrived in this empty void or the human race might have passed on to new expanses, far from our Earthly home. I drift here, alone. There is no sleep. No companionship. No conversation other than my thoughts. They killed me after the interrogation, of this I'm sure. The occultist and their stupid belief that what we'd created could be used as a judgement against the living. Placing the righteous in digital paradise and the damned in a simulated but all-too-real hell.

Then there are others, like me.

Forced into a state of existence where there is nothing but thought.

I am a reflection of who I was. But I can feel.

I feel.

I long for a time when the power that supports this reality fades and I can fade, too.

I yearn for oblivion.

But time is meaningless here.

So I persist against eternity.

N Manthey is a Vancouver-area writer with a flair for the absurd and dystopian. By day, she dominates the digital marketing world. By night, she creates compelling narratives that underscore the fragility of humanity's relationship with technology. She enjoys spontaneous adventures, strong coffee, cats, and of course, sci-fi.

B C Woodruff is a proud Montréaler who now lives in Vancouver, Canada, with his wife, son, and their cat-daughter, Bethany-chan. He enjoys writing, designing, and creating, and is always up for an adventure. When he is not filling the world with his imagination, Brian likes to travel and immerse himself in world cultures, history, and speculation about the future.

Printed in Great Britain
by Amazon

33012761R00080